D0344779

Copyright © 1985 by Shirley Hughes.
First published in Great Britain in 1985 by Walker Books Ltd.

Printed in Italy.
First U.S. edition published in 1985. 1   2   3   4   5   6   7   8   9   10

Library of Congress Cataloging in Publication Data

Hughes, Shirley.
    When we went to the park.
    Summary: A little girl and her grandpa count the things they see
during a walk in the park.
    1. Children's stories, English.   [1. Grandfathers—Fiction.
2. Parks—Fiction. 3. Counting]   I. Title.   PZ7.H87395Wh 1985
[E]   84-12624
ISBN 0-688-04204-X

When We
Went to the Park

Shirley Hughes

LOTHROP, LEE & SHEPARD BOOKS
NEW YORK

When Grandpa and I put on our coats

and went to the park...

we saw one black cat sitting on a wall,

two big girls licking ice-creams,

three ladies chatting on a bench,

four babies in buggies,

five children playing in the sandpile,

six runners running,

seven dogs chasing one another,

eight boys kicking a ball,

nine ducks swimming on the pond,

ten birds swooping in the sky,

and so many leaves that I couldn't
count them all.

On the way back we saw the
black cat again.

Then we went home for supper.